The Best of West

The Best of West

Selected Verse of Colin West

Hutchinson

London Sydney Auckland Johannesburg

To K.A. & D.F.

First published in Great Britain in 1990 by
Hutchinson Children's Books
An imprint of Century Hutchinson Ltd
20 Vauxhall Bridge Road, London SW1V 2SA

Century Hutchinson Australia (Pty) Ltd
20 Alfred Street, Milsons Point, Sydney 2061, Australia

Century Hutchinson New Zealand Limited
32–34 View Road, PO Box 40–086, Glenfield, Auckland 10

Century Hutchinson South Africa (Pty) Ltd
PO Box 337, Bergvlei, South Africa

Typeset by Speedset Ltd, Ellesmere Port
Printed and bound in Great Britain by
Butler and Tanner Ltd, Frome and London

All poems first published by Hutchinson Children's Books in *Not to be Taken Seriously* (1982), *A Step in the Wrong Direction* (1984), *It's Funny When You Look at It* (1984), *A Moment in Rhyme* (1987), *What Would You do with a Wobble-dee-woo?* (1988) and *Between the Sun, the Moon and Me* (1990)

British Library Cataloguing in Publication Data
West, Colin
The best of West.
I. Title
821.914

ISBN 0–09–173587–4

Contents

Introduction

There are unclaimed poems floating all around, just waiting for someone to catch them.

They can come when you least expect.

On a bus. In the bath. Half-way through a football match.

And if you haven't a pen and paper handy, they may flit out of your mind, and into somebody else's.

The poem may end up in the Himalayas. Or Muswell Hill. Or Ashby-de-la-Zouch.

That's how it goes.

Anyway, here are some rhymes I've managed to catch over the years. I hope you have fun reading them . . .

Colin West

Funny
Folk

My Uncle is a Baronet

My uncle is a baronet,
He sleeps beside the hearth,
And likes to play the clarinet
Whilst sitting in the bath.

Deborah, Deborah

Deborah, Deborah, Deborah is it
Possible for you to visit
Far-off lands that are exquisite,
And though I wouldn't *force* you,
I hear the Outer Hebrides
Are beautiful, so Deborah please,
Ride off upon my zebra, he's
Just waiting for a horseshoe!

My Obnoxious Brother Bobby

My obnoxious brother Bobby
Has a most revolting hobby;
There, behind the garden wall is
Where he captures creepy-crawlies.

Grannies, aunts and baby cousins
Come to our house in their dozens,
But they disappear discreetly
When they see him smiling sweetly.

For they know, as he approaches,
In his pockets are cockroaches,
Spiders, centipedes and suchlike;
All of which they do not much like.

As they head towards the lobby,
Bidding fond farewells to Bobby,
How they wish he'd change his habits
And keep guinea pigs or rabbits.

But their wishes are quite futile,
For he thinks that bugs are cute. I'll
Finish now, but just remind you:
Bobby could be right behind you!

In One Ear and Out the Other

When Miss Tibbs talks
To my dear brother,
It goes in one ear
And out the other;
And when she shouts,
He seldom hears,
The words just whistle
Through his ears.

His ears are big,
(You must've seen 'em)
But he's got nothing
In between 'em.
The truth, Miss Tibbs,
Is hard to face:
His head is full
Of empty space.

She Likes to Swim Beneath the Sea

She likes to swim beneath the sea
And wear her rubber flippers,
She likes to dance outrageously
And wake up all the kippers.

Lanky Lee and Lindy Lou

Said Lanky Lee
To Lindy Lou,
'Please let me run
Away with you!'
But Lou replied
With frustration:
'You've got no
Imagination,
For that is all,
Dear Lanky Lee,
That ever runs
Away with *me*!'

Muriel

Muriel, Muriel,
You're oh so mercurial,
One moment you're up,
The next moment you're down.
Your moods are not durable,
You seem quite incurable –
For now you are laughing,
But soon you will frown.

My Sister Sybil

Sipping soup, my sister Sybil
Seems inclined to drool and dribble.
If it wasn't for this foible,
Meal-times would be more enjoyable!

Mavis Morris

Mavis Morris was a girl
Who liked to pirouette and twirl.
One day upon a picnic, she
Whirled enthusiastically.
A hundred times she spun around –
And bore herself into the ground.

The Unlikely Mermaid

Please pardon my asking you, Irene,
But why do you sit on the stair,
As seaward you gaze out the window
As though there were somebody there?

The ocean is calling me
For to return,
For I was a mermaid
Before you were born.

Please pardon my ignorance, Irene,
I must seem remarkably dim.
I don't understand – *you* a mermaid?
I know for a fact you can't swim.

A mermaid does other things
Other than float,
Like singing a shanty
By clearing her throat.

Please pardon my doubting you, Irene,
I cannot believe what you say.
Your skin hasn't scales and your body
Resembles a fish in no way.

I wouldn't expect you to
Think it is true;
For I'm not a fire-breathing
Dragon like you.

Norman Norton's Nostrils

Oh, Norman Norton's nostrils
Are powerful and strong;
Hold on to your belongings
If he should come along.

And do not ever let him
Inhale with all his might,
Or else your pens and pencils
Will disappear from sight.

Right up his nose they'll vanish;
Your future will be black.
Unless he gets the sneezes
You'll *never* get them back!

When Betty Eats Spaghetti

When Betty eats spaghetti,
She slurps, she slurps, she slurps.
And when she's finished slurping,
She burps, she burps, she burps.

My Sister Joan

I'm sad to say my sister Joan
Has confiscated my trombone,
And so, to get my *own* back,
Tonight, as she's tucked up in bed,
I'll play my violin instead ...
Till I get my trombone back.

An Alphabet of Horrible Habits

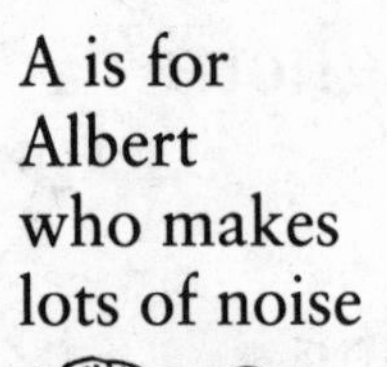

A is for
Albert
who makes
lots of noise

B is for
Bertha
who bullies
the boys

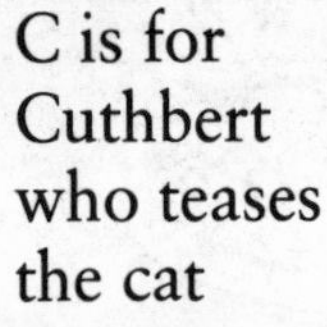

C is for
Cuthbert
who teases
the cat

D is for
Dilys
whose singing
is flat

E is for
Enid
Who's never
on time

F is for
Freddy
who's covered
in slime

G is for
Gilbert
who never
says thanks

H is for
Hannah
who plans to
rob banks

I is for
Ivy
who slams
the front
door

J is for
Jacob
whose jokes
are a bore

K is for
Kenneth
who won't
wash his face

L is for
Lucy
who cheats
in a race

M is for
Maurice
who gobbles
his food

N is for
Nora
who runs
about nude

O is for
Olive
who treads
on your toes

P is for
Percy
who *will*
pick his nose

Q is for
Queenie
who won't tell
the truth

R is for
Rupert
who's rather
uncouth

S is for
Sibyl
who bellows
and bawls

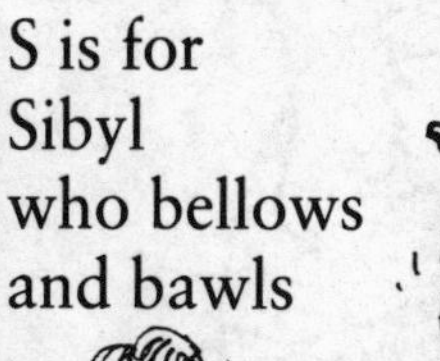

T is for
Thomas
who scribbles
on walls

U is for
Una
who fidgets
too much

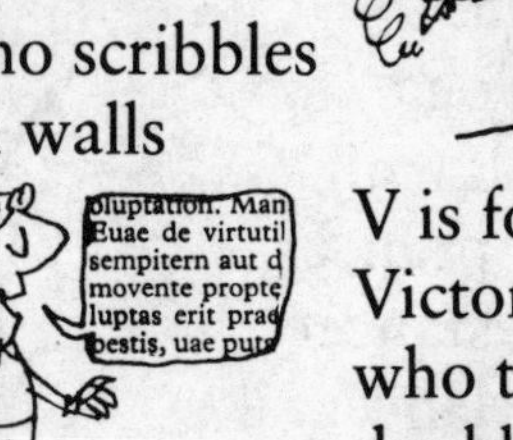

V is for
Victor
who talks
double Dutch

W is for
Wilma
who won't wipe
her feet

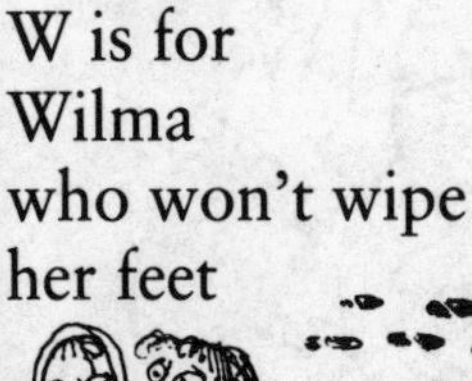

X is for
Xerxes
who never
is neat

Y is for
Yorick
who's vain
as can be

and Z is for
Zoe
who doesn't
love me.

Nora the Nibbler

Nora nibbles like a rabbit,
It's a funny sort of habit.
First a carrot she will pick up,
Nibble it, then start to hiccup,
After which she'll start to nibble
Once more at her vegetibble.

O That Ogre!

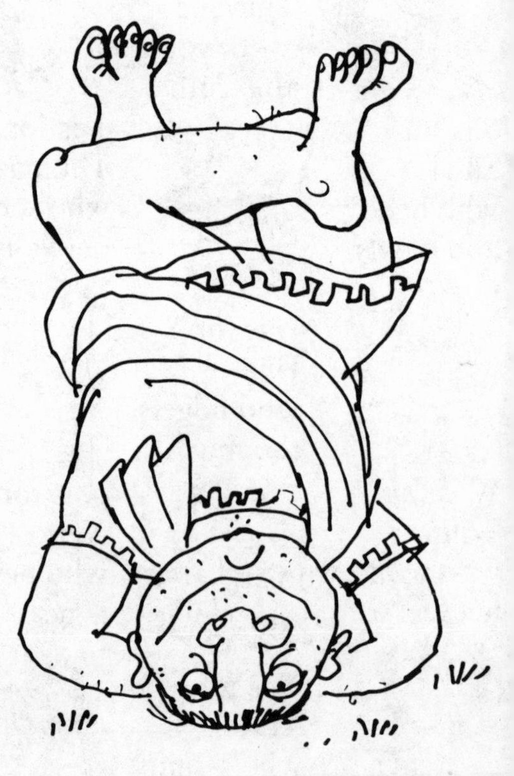

O that Ogre,
In a toga,
Doing yoga
On my lawn!
What a prancer,
What a stancer,
Fattest dancer
Ever born!
Watch him tumble,
Feel him fumble,
Hear him mumble
On till dawn:
'I'm an Ogre
In a toga,
Doing yoga
On your lawn!'

Rodney Reid

In his bathtub Rodney Reid is
Making quite a mess,
Thus disproving Archimedes'
Principle,* no less.

(Note the body in this case is
But a boy of four,
Yet the fluid it displaces
Covers all the floor.)

*When a body is immersed in water, its apparent loss of weight is equal to the weight of the water displaced. So there!

Clumsy Clarissa

Clarissa did the washing up:
She smashed a plate and chipped a cup,
And dropped a glass and cracked a mug,
Then pulled the handle off a jug.
She couldn't do much worse, you'd think,
But then she went and broke the sink.

Adolphus

Adolphus is despicable –
Before the day begins,
To prove that I am kickable,
He kicks me in the shins.

Tout Ensemble

Paula pounds the grand piano,
Vera plays the violin,
Percival provides percussion
On an empty biscuit tin.
Connie plays the concertina,
Mervyn strums the mandolin;
When you put them all together –
They make one almighty din.

Nicola

I'm glad I'm not
Like Nicola,
Who may look sweet
As honey.
But even if you
Tickle her,
She doesn't find
It funny.

Michael

Michael likes 'Michael',
He doesn't like 'Mike'.
He rides on a 'cycle',
and *not* on a 'bike'.
He doesn't like 'Mickey',
He doesn't like 'Mick';
Don't offer a 'bikky' –
It might make him sick.

Veronica

Adventurous Veronica
Upon her yacht *Japonica*
Is sailing to Dominica.
She blows her old harmonica
Each night beneath the spinnaker,
And dreams of seeing Monica,
Her sister, in Dominica.

Curious Creatures

The Pig

The table manners of the pig
Leave much to be desired.
His appetite is always big,
His talk is uninspired.

And if you ask him out to dine
You'll only ask him once,
Unless you like to see a swine
Who gobbles as he grunts.

The Crab

The crab has still far to evolve
Till he attains perfection,
For still, it seems, he cannot solve
The question of direction.
So when he goes from 'A' to 'B'
Along the ocean tideways,
He also visits 'C' and 'D'
Because he travels sideways!

Octopus

Last Saturday I came across
Most nonchalant an octopus;
I couldn't help but make a fuss,
And shook him by the tentacle.

He seemed to find it all a bore
And asked me, 'Have we met before?
I'm sorry, but I can't be sure,
You chaps all look identical.'

The Wild Boar

The features of the porcupine
I'm glad to say are his, not mine;
Likewise the bandicoot has got
A face I do not like a lot,
And furthermore the chimpanzee
Has looks that don't appeal to me.
As for the vicious vampire bat,
I'm thankful I don't look like *that*;
And what about the octopus?
Of him I am not envious!
In fact, there is no other beast
I'd care to look like in the least;
No fellow creature comes to mind
With looks so noble and refined.
It's evident that though a boar,
I've much I should be grateful for.

The Grizzly Bear

The grizzly bear is horrible,
His habits quite deplorable.
He's not the sort of beast
I'd ask to tea.
The reason for my quibble is
I think *Ursus horribilis*
Looks just the sort of beast
Who might eat *me*.

Glow-worm

I know a worried glow-worm,
I wonder what the matter is?
He seems so glum and gloomy,
Perhaps he needs new batteries!

The Axolotl

The axolotl acts a little
Fishily at times.
In Mexico, some gills he'll grow,
But when in cooler climes,
Upon dry land a salamander
He may choose to be,
Though why he should and how he could
Is still not clear to me!

Geraldine Giraffe

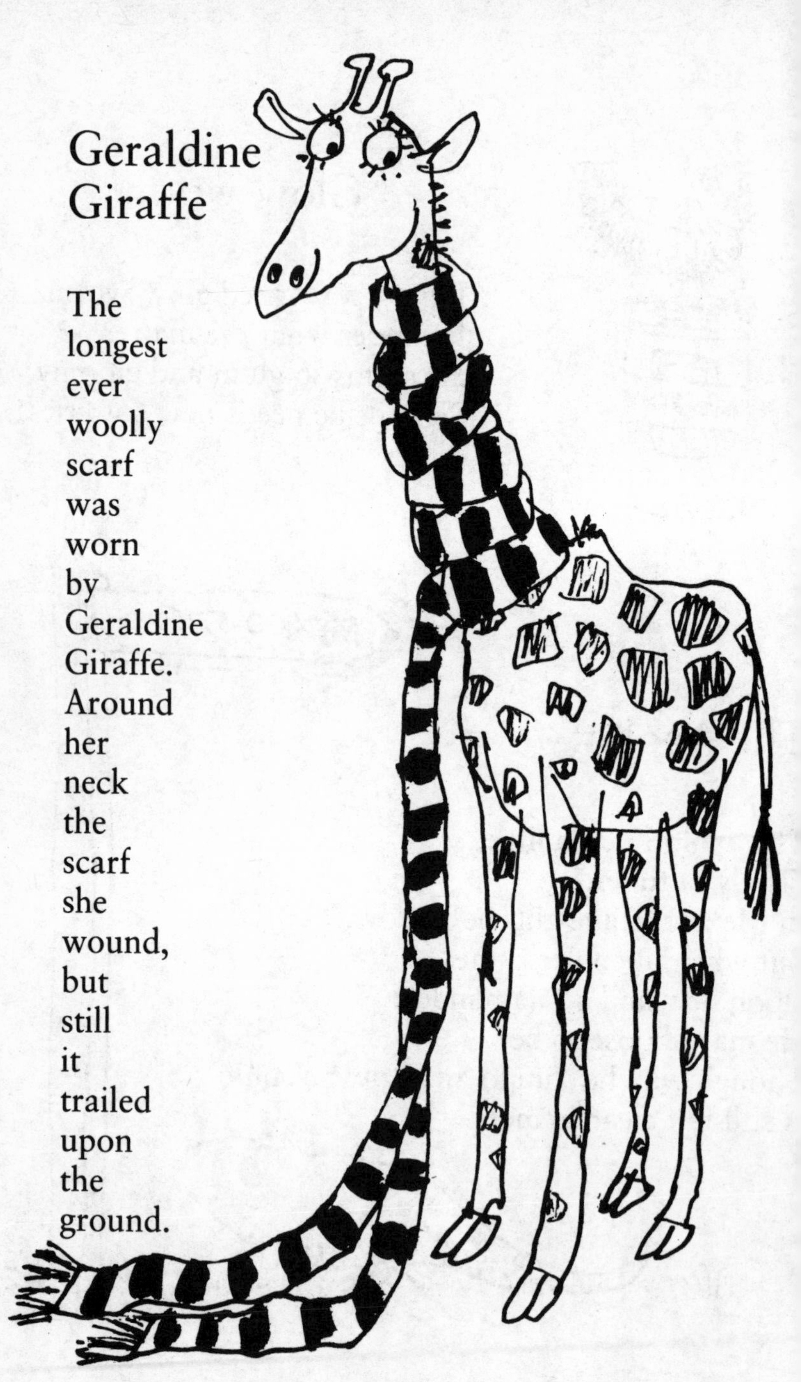

The
longest
ever
woolly
scarf
was
worn
by
Geraldine
Giraffe.
Around
her
neck
the
scarf
she
wound,
but
still
it
trailed
upon
the
ground.

Pangolin

This disrespectful pangolin
Reclines upon a pillow,
And plays upon a mandolin
Made from an armadillo.

To sing his songs is his intent,
At nineteen to the dozen,
And so he strums an instrument
That used to be his cousin.

Our Hippopotamus

We thought a lively pet to keep
Might be a hippopotamus.
Now see him sitting in a heap,
And notice at the bottom – us.

The Tortoise

The tortoise has a tendency
To live beyond his prime,
Thus letting his descendants see
How *they* will look in time.

The Scorpion

Spiders, scorpions and mites
Are not the pleasantest of sights;
The scorpion, especially,
Does not endear itself to me.
Yet, looks aside, I must confess,
If ever I'm about to dress,
And notice one inside my shoe,
It's not as bad as failing to.

A Penguin's Life

A penguin's life is cold and wet
And always in a muddle,
A penguin's feet are wet and damp
And often in a puddle.

O how ironic! O how absurd!
A penguin cannot fly about
Like any other bird.
O how monotonous,
I'd so much like to be
A big fat hippopotamus
Upon the rolling sea!

A penguin's nose is frozen stiff
And feels just like an icicle,
A penguin has to be content
To live without a bicycle.

O how ironic! O how absurd!
That I'm not supersonic
Like any other bird.
O the frustration,
I'd so much like to hear
The trains at Tooting Station
And the trams at Belvedere!

Good Homes for Kittens

Who'd like a Siamese?
Yes, please.

An Angora?
I'd adora.

A Tabby?
Ma'be.

A Black and White?
All right.

A Tortoiseshell?
Oh, very well.

A Manx?
No *thanx!*

The Auk

How very awkward for the auk
To be resigned to merely squawk,
And never say a single word
To anyone but fellow bird.

And yet, supposing we could teach
The auk the art of human speech,
If we should ever ask him out,
Whatever would we talk about?

Auntie Agnes's Cat

My Auntie Agnes has a cat.
I do not like to tell her that
Its body seems a little large
(With lots of stripes for camouflage).
Its teeth and claws are also larger
Than they ought to be. A rajah
Gave her the kitten, I recall,
When she was stationed in Bengal.
But that was many years ago,
And kittens are inclined to grow.
So now she has a fearsome cat –
But I don't like to tell her that.

Chameleons

Chameleons are seldom seen,
They're red, they're orange, then they're green.
They're one of nature's strangest sights,
Their colours change like traffic lights!

Anteater

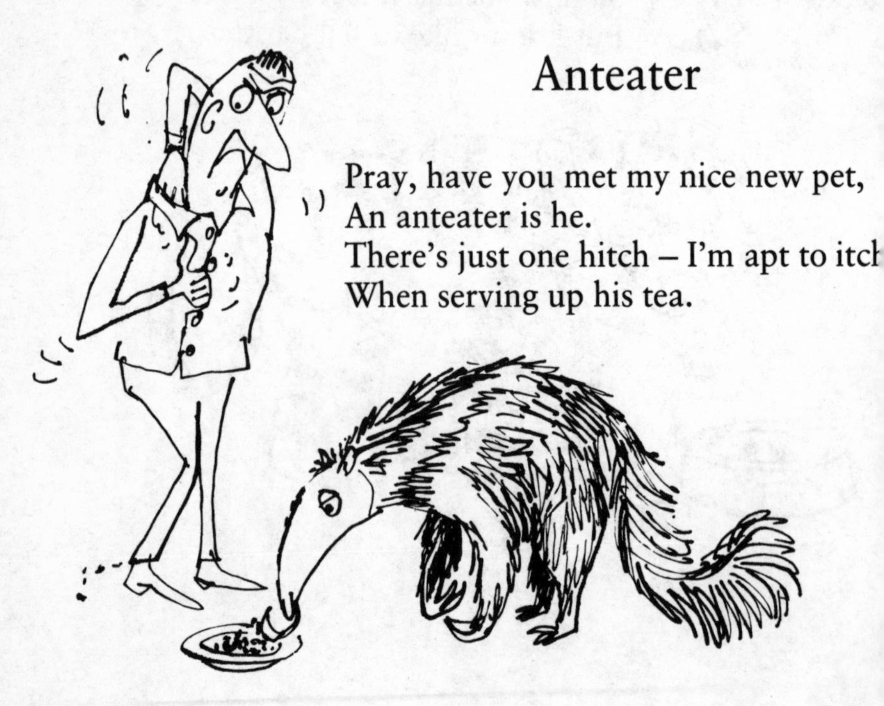

Pray, have you met my nice new pet,
An anteater is he.
There's just one hitch – I'm apt to itc
When serving up his tea.

The Sloth

The sloth may smile,
The sloth may frown.
It's hard to tell –
he's upside down!

Proboscis Monkey

Proboscis monkey, I suppose
You've grown accustomed to your nose.
But what precisely did you do
To get that nose to grow on you?

The Orang-utan

The closest relative of man
They say, is the orang-utan;
And when I look at Grandpapa,
I realize how right they are.

O Rattlesnake, Rattlesnake

O Rattlesnake, Rattlesnake,
What noise does your rattle make?
O won't you please rattle
Your rattle for me?

(*So the Rattlesnake rattled its rattle.*)

O Rattlesnake, Rattlesnake,
Pray, doesn't your rattle ache?
You've rattled your rattle
Since twenty to three.

(*Still the Rattlesnake rattled its rattle.*)

O Rattlesnake, Rattlesnake,
Please no more your rattle shake.
O won't you stop rattling
Your rattle, pray do!

(*But the Rattlesnake rattled its rattle.*)

O Rattlesnake, Rattlesnake,
For you and your rattle's sake,
You'd better stop rattling
Your rattle. Thank you!

(*So the Rattlesnake bit me instead.*)

Tricky Tonguetwisters

Willoughby the Wallaby

I want to be a wallaby,
A wallaby like Willoughby.
When *will* I be a wallaby
Like Willoughby the wallaby?

Cynthia Smith

Cynthia Smith has still not thought
A single thought since Thursday,
Since Cynthia Smith is not the sort
To think a single sort of thought.

Kitty and the Kittiwake

Did Kitty wake
The kittiwake,
Or did the kittiwake
Wake Kitty?

Adelaide

Adelaide is up a ladder.
Adelaide's an adder-upper.
She's an addled adder-upper,
Adding adders up a ladder.

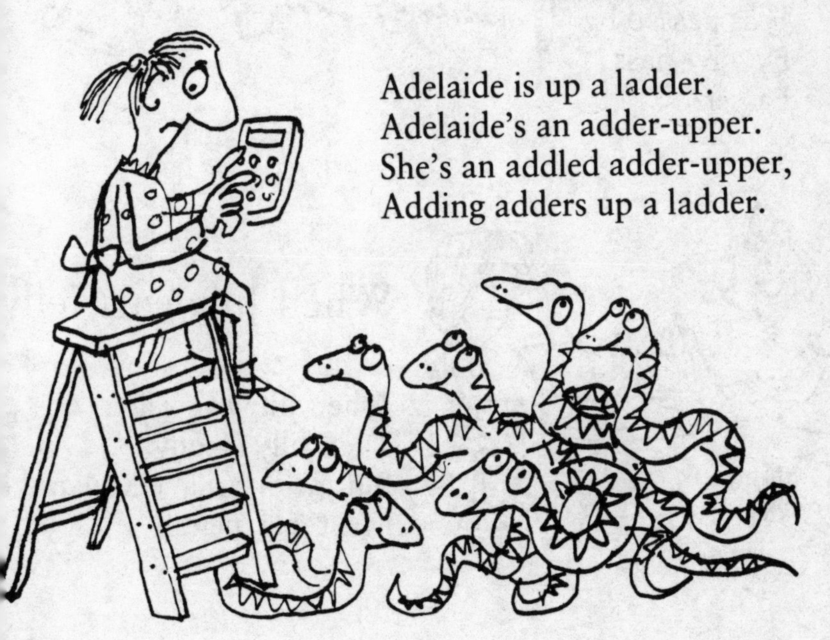

Passers-by

A passer-by
Was passing by
A by-pass,
And passing by
The by-pass,
A passer-by
Passed by:
By passing by
A by-pass
As a passer-by
Passed by,
A passer-by
Was passed by
By a by-pass
Passer-by.

When Jilly eats Jelly

When Jilly eats jelly,
Then Jilly is jolly.
But melons make Melanie
Most melancholy.

Ethel Read a Book

Ethel read, Ethel read,
Ethel read a book.
Ethel read a book in bed,
She read a book on Ethelred.
The book that Ethel read in bed,
(The book on Ethelred) was red.
The book was red that Ethel read,
In bed on Ethelred.

Juggler Jim

I'm Jim and I juggle a jug and a jar
And junkets and jelly and jam.
With jovial, joyful and jocular jests,
How jolly a jester I am!

Please Pass the Parsley, Percival

Please pass the parsley, Percival,
Please pass the parsley, Percy,
The parsley, Percival, please pass,
Please, Percy, pass the parsley.

If a Ghoul is Fond of Goulash

If a ghoul is fond of goulash,
Is the ghoul a little foolish,
Should he feel, if full of goulash,
As a ghoul he's not so ghoulish?

King Canute Cannot

King Canute cannot k-nit,
K-nit Canute cannot;
King Canute cannot k-nit,
King Canute cannot!

Superciliousness

Some say they think that 'super'
Is not the thing to say:
They say that super's silly;
Oh, supercilious they!

Beetroot

Be true to me, beetroot, be true,
And I will too be true;
But beetroot, if you be untrue,
I'll be untrue to you.

Scarecrows

The trouble with scarecrows
Is that they *don't* scare crows,
And don't seem to care crows
Are not scared by scarecrows.

A Cymbal for the Singer

Here's a cymbal for the singer
With a thimble on his finger:
See the singer with a thimble
On his finger thump the cymbal!

Mr Lott's Allotment

Mr Lott's allotment
Meant a lot to Mr Lott.
Now Mr Lott is missed a lot
On Mr Lott's allotment.

Toboggan

To begin to toboggan, first buy a toboggan,
But don't buy too big a toboggan.
(A too big a toboggan is not a toboggan
To buy to begin to toboggan.)

Moments with Monsters

The Flipper-Flopper Bird

O have you never ever heard
Of the Flipper-Flopper Bird?
O have you never seen his teeth,
Two above and one beneath?

O have you never known the thrill
Of stroking his enormous bill?
O have you never taken tea
With him sitting up a tree?

O have you never seen him hop
As he goes a-flip, a-flop?
O have you never heard his cry?
No, you've never? Nor have I.

The Ogglewop

The Ogglewop is tall and wide,
And though he looks quite passive,
He's crammed with boys and girls inside,
– That's why he is so massive!

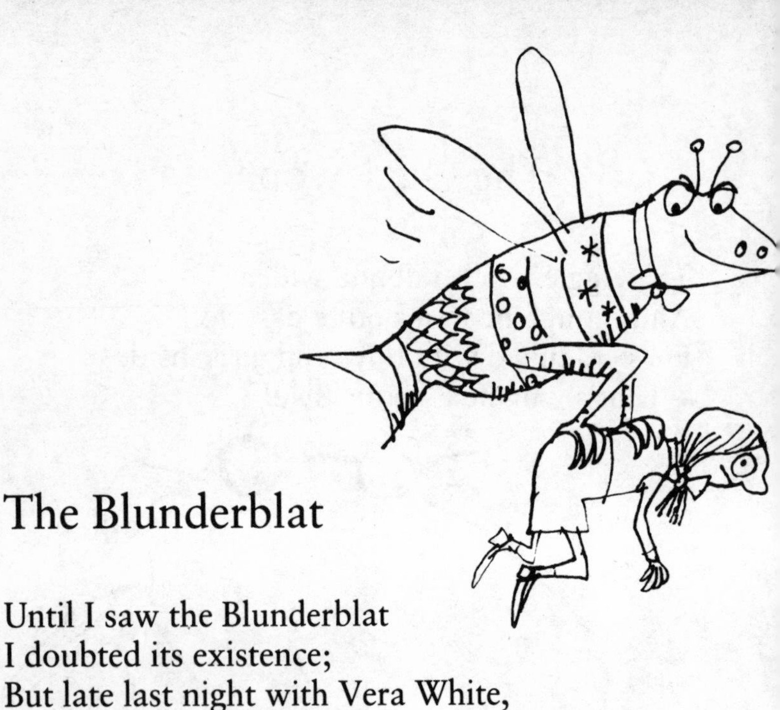

The Blunderblat

Until I saw the Blunderblat
I doubted its existence;
But late last night with Vera White,
I saw one in the distance.

I reached for my binoculars,
Which finally I focused;
I watched it rise into the skies,
Like some colossal locust.

I heard it hover overhead,
I shrieked as it came nearer;
I held my breath, half scared to death,
And prayed it might take Vera.

And so it did, I'm glad to say,
Without too much resistance.
Dear Blunderblat, I'm sorry that
I doubted your existence.

The Glump

Your life may be in jeopardy,
The Glump is on its way.
Its legs are long and leopardy,
It pounces on its prey.

It bears some similarity,
You'll notice, to a bird.
Its beak is pink and parroty,
Its cry is quite absurd.

I think the Glump is easily
Our most obnoxious beast.
Its teeth are white and weasely,
And waiting for a feast.

You'll reel and writhe in agony,
Unless you disappear.
Its skin is dry and dragony ...
Oh dear, the Glump is here.

Monstrous Imagination

'Mummy, can't you see the monster
Hiding by the curtain?'
'Why Joseph dear, there's nothing there,
Of that I am quite certain.
The monster that you *think* you see
Within the shadows lurking,
Is your imagination, dear,
Which overtime is working.'

Thus reassured, Joe went to sleep;
His mother's explanation
Seemed only right: Beasts of the Night
Are mere imagination.
And sound his slumber was until
In dreams the monster met him.
Now Joe we'll miss, for last night his
'Imagination' ate him.

The Gobblegulp

The Gobblegulp is most uncouth,
In his mouth is just one tooth,
He gobbles food and gulps Ribena
Like a living vacuum cleaner.
He has a great big bulging belly
That wobbles when he walks like jelly,
But what I like about him least
Is that he is a noisy beast,
For when he eats an apple crumble,
His tummy starts to roll and rumble;
I often hear a noise and wonder,
'Was that a Gobblegulp – or thunder?'

The Furbelow

The Furbelow will eat your home,
From the floorboards to the rafters;
Then, having scoffed the furniture,
Will eat you up for afters.

The Finisher-Upper

To demolish a dinner
Or diminish a supper,
Why don't you call for
The Finisher-Upper?

Watch him demolish
And watch him diminish
Any old left-over food
He can finish.

His performance is always
So perfect and polished:
Suppers diminished
And dinners demolished!

Dotty
Ditties

Pretty Polly Perkins

'Pretty Polly Perkins,
What would you like to eat?
Greengages and gherkins,
Or marmalade and meat?

Cakes and Coca Cola,
Or chocolate and ham?
Grapes and Gorgonzola,
Or sausages and jam?'

'Thank you, sir', says Polly,
'But what would please me most
Would be a lemon lolly
Upon a slice of toast.'

The Trouble with Boy

The trouble with boys is
They make funny noises;
They rage and they riot,
And seldom are quiet.
They seem extra naughty
With folk over forty,
And do things they oughtn't
To persons important.

Dressing Gown

Why do people
I'm addressing
Frown
When I've got on
My dressing
Gown?
And some give me
A dressing
Down
When I've got on
My dressing
Gown?

The Hole Truth

If it takes three men to dig one hole
Two hours and one minute,
How long would six men take to dig
A hole exactly twice as big,
And could you push them in it?

Inquisitiveness

Please, how does one spell *definite*?
Has it a double *f* in it?

Please, how old was Euripides?
And where are the Antipodes?

Please, where does one find phosphorus?
And how big is the Bosporus?

Please, why are you so furious?
Do tell me, I'm *so* curious.

Amongst My Friends

Amongst my friends
I number some
Sixteen or so
Who dance.
Some like to do
The rhumba, some
Will waltz if they've
The chance;
And even in
Their slumber, some
Will foxtrot in
A trance.
But as for me,
I'm cumbersome,
And all I do
Is prance.

The Loofah

The loofah feels he can't relax,
For something is amiss:
He scratches other people's backs,
But no one scratches *his*.

What do Teachers Dream of?

What do teachers dream of,
In mountains and in lowlands?
They dream of exclamation marks,
Full stops and semi-colons!

Putting the Shot

Tomorrow I may put the shot,
Or on the other hand, may not;
For yesterday I put the shot,
But where I put it, I forgot.

Luke

Luke's a lisper.
I've heard a whisper,
He's at his zenith
Playing tennith.

Custard

I like it thin without a skin,
My sister likes it thicker.
But thick or thin, when tucking in,
I'm noisier and quicker.

Hither and Thither

Hither and thither,
She plays on the zither,
Her music is ever so mellow;
But don't stop and dither,
Just look who is with her –
Her husband who's playing the cello.

He scratches and screeches,
The high notes he reaches
Sound more like a cat being sat on;
Conductors throw peaches
When passing, and each is
Soon seen to be breaking his baton.

Both crotchet and quaver
Seem somehow to savour
A key neither major nor minor,
And if I were braver,
I'd ask him a favour,
'Why *don't* you please practise in China?'

My Auntie

My auntie who lives in
Llanfairpwllgwyngyllgogerych-
  wyrndrobwllllantysiliogogogoch
Has asked me to stay.

But unfortunately
Llanfairpwllgwyngyllgogerych-
  wyrndrobwllllantysiliogogogoch
Is a long, long way away.

Will I ever go to
Llanfairpwllgwyngyllgogerych-
  wyrndrobwllllantysiliogogogoch?
It's difficult to say.

Bed of Nails

I sleep upon a bed of nails.
I must confess it never fails
To help me get a good night's rest,
And, overall, I'm most impressed!

Etymology for Entomologists

O Longitude and Latitude,
I always get them muddled;
(I'm sure they'd be offended, though,
To think that I'm befuddled).

O Isobars and Isotherms,
Please tell me how they differ;
(For competition 'twixt the two,
I hear, could not be stiffer).

O Seraphim and Cherubim,
Don't care for one another;
(Although for me it's difficult
To tell one from the other).

O Stalagmites and Stalactites,
Whenever I peruse 'em,
Though one grows up, and one grows down,
I can't help but confuse 'em.

Rhubarb, Rhubarb

'Rhubarb, rhubarb, what a lot
Of lovely rhubarb you have got
Growing in your rhubarb plot.
Rhubarb, rhubarb, rhubarb.'

'Rhubarb, rhubarb, thank you so.
Rhubarb's all I ever grow;
And I *talk* it too, you know,
Rhubarb, rhubarb, rhubarb.'

A Wisp of a Wasp

I'm a wisp of a wasp with a worry,
I'm hiding somewhere in Surrey,
I've just bit upon
The fat sit upon
Of the King – so I left in a hurry!

Trampoline

I've got a hundred pounds to spend, and I am really keen,
If you could only serve me, miss, to buy this trampoline.
I'm sorry to disturb you, miss, I hate to intervene,
But could you for a moment, please, put down your magazine?

Orange Silver Sausage

Some words I've studied for a time,
Like *orange, silver, sausage*;
But as for finding them a rhyme,
I'm at a total lossage.

Because It Was There

One of the very cleverest
Of men who conquered Everest
Gave this reply when questioned why:
'Because it was there.'

I hope that this example shows
Just why I punched you on the nose.
If questioned why I shall reply:
'******* ** *** ***** '.

A Pelican in Delhi Can

A pelican in Delhi can
Spend his whole life alone.
But an elephant in Delhi can't
Be often on his own.

Rolling Down a Hill

I’m rolling
rolling
rolling
down

I’m rolling
down a
hill.

I’m rolling
rolling
rolling
down

I’m rolling
down it
still.

I’m rolling
rolling
rolling
down

I’m rolling
down a
hill

I’m rolling
rolling
down

But now
I’m feeling
ill.

Petunia's Pet

Petunia's pet is a pet-and-a-half,
Some say it's a tapir, some say a giraffe.
Some say it is neither, some say it is both,
But Pet doesn't care and she's plighted her troth.

Pogo Stick

Upon my pogo stick I pounce

And out of school I homeward bounce.

I bounce so high, how my heart pounds

Until at last I'm out of bounds.

Short Words

Short words that we use, such as *bee, bat* or *bird*,
Go under a name quite inapt and absurd;
No wonder this adjective seldom is heard,
For *monosyllabic*, I fear, is the word.

French Accents

Acute, or Grave or Circumflex,
In France we use all three;
And sometimes too, Cedilla who
Is found beneath the C.

Vicious Verses

Cousin Jane

Yesterday my cousin Jane
Said she was an aeroplane,
But I wanted further proof –
So I pushed her off the roof.

Malcolm

Let us pray for cousin Malcolm,
Smothered as he was in talcum;
He sneezed whilst seasoning his chowder
And vanished in a puff of powder.

Laurence

Laurence by a lion was mauled,
And it's left us quite appalled.
He had on his 'Sunday best';
Now he's gone and torn his vest.

When Rover Passed Over

When Rover died, my sister cried;
I tried my best to calm her.
I said 'We'll have him mummified,
I know a good embalmer.'

And so we packed the wretched pup
Into a wicker basket.
We duly had him bandaged up,
And kept him in a casket.

Now Rover we will not forget,
Though he is but a dummy.
For though we've lost a faithful pet,
We've gained an extra Mummy!

Percy and the Python

Poor Percy met a python once
When walking in the jungle,
And being something of a dunce,
He made a fatal bungle.

He went to stroke its scaly skin
As from a tree it dangled.
Alas, before he could begin,
The python left him strangled.

It then went on to crush to pulp
His body, very neatly;
Until, with one enormous gulp,
It swallowed him completely.

This story shows that such a snake
Should always be avoided.
So do not make the same mistake
As this unthinking boy did!

Betty

Wearing all her diamonds, Betty
Rode too fast along the jetty.
How I wish she'd not been reckless;
We could not retrieve her necklace.

Kitty

Isn't it a
Dreadful pity
What became of
Dreamy Kitty,
Noticing the
Moon above her,
Not
the
missing
man-hole
cover?

Misguided Marcus

Marcus met an alligator
Half a mile from the equator;
Marcus, ever optimistic,
Said, 'This beast is not sadistic.'
Marcus even claimed the creature
'Has a kind and loving nature'.
In that case, pray tell me, Marcus,
Why have you become a carcass?

Little Barbara

Little Barbara went to Scarborough,
Just to buy a candelabra.
At the harbour a bear ate Barbara.
Don't you find that most macabre?

The Greedy Alligator

I have a rather greedy pet,
A little alligator;
When he my younger sister met,
He opened wide and ate her.

But soon he learned that he was wrong
To eat the child in question,
For he felt bad before too long,
And suffered indigestion.

This story seems to prove to me
That he who rudely gobbles
Will soon regret his gluttony
And get the collywobbles.

Aunt Carol

Making vinegar, Aunt Carol
Fell into her brimming barrel.
As she drowned, my teardrops
trickled;
Now she's permanently pickled.

Kate

In the kitchen Kate went tripping
Landing in a vat of dripping.
When the Red Cross came to fetch her,
Kate kept slipping off the stretcher.

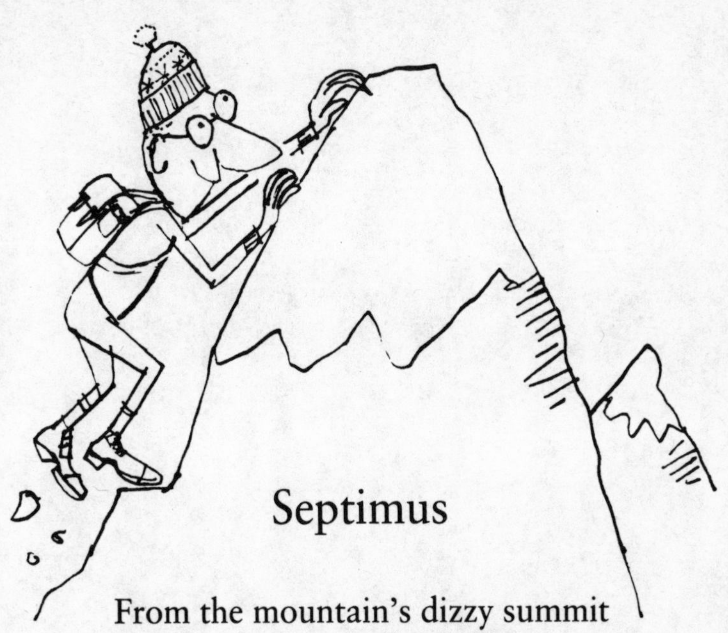

Septimus

From the mountain's dizzy summit
Septimus is soon to plummet.
This, alas, will prove the last time
He goes climbing as a pastime.

Auntie Babs

untie Babs became besotted
Vith her snake, so nicely spotted,
Jnaware that pets so mottled
ike to leave their keepers throttled.

Nothing but Nonsense

Tomorrow I've Given Up Hope

I've sailed all the seas in a bathtub,
And climbed all the mountains with rope,
I've flown in the skies
With soap in my eyes,
But tomorrow I've given up hope.

I've picked all the world's rarest flowers,
And seen the uncommonest trees,
I've paddled in ponds,
And made friends with fronds,
But tomorrow still quite eludes me.

I never have *seen* a tomorrow,
I've never been able to say:
'Tomorrow has come,
The bumble bees hum,
Tomorrow's come early today!'

Where Raindrops Plop

Where raindrops plop in muddy streams,
And thunder shakes the trees,
Where pigs who've played in football teams
Go home in twos and threes;
Where harpists pluck at mournful strings,
And sadness fills the air,
Where creep a hundred hairy things,
I think that I'll go there.

Where green leaves lie upon the lakes,
And gentle mists descend,
Where noises that the hedgehog makes
Seem only to offend;
Where darkness hangs above the fields,
And moles are made to roam,
Where stands the sett the badger builds,
That's where I'll call my home.

O How I Hate the Poet!

The purpose of a porpoise,
Or a turtle or a tortoise,
Or a salamander well I understand.
The reason for a rumpus,
Or a camel or a compass,
Or a saxophone is plain to any man.

The meaning of a mangle,
Or a congruent triangle,
Or a hemisphere is very clear to see,
But one thing I must mention,
Quite beyond my comprehension,
Is the problem that the poet poses me.

A poet spends his hours
Sat in sofas sniffing flowers,
And writing rhymes as silly as can be.
Just watch him with his poodles,
I would give a hundred roubles
To someone who could explain his use to me.

The Darkest and Dingiest Dungeon

Down in the darkest and dingiest dungeon,
Far from the tiniest twinkle of stars,
Far from the whiff of a wonderful luncheon,
Far from the murmur of motoring cars,
Far from the habits of rabbits and weasels,
Far from the merits of ferrets and stoats,
Far from the danger of mumps or of measles,
Far from the fashions of fabulous coats,
Far from the turn of a screw in a socket,
Far from the fresh frozen food in the fridge,
Far from the fluff in my dufflecoat pocket,
Far from the bite of a mischievous midge,
Far from the hole in my humble umbrella,
Far from my hat as it hangs in the hall,
I sit here alone with myself in the cellar,
I *do* so like getting away from it all!

Barge Pole

Poetry?
I wouldn't touch it with a barge pole.

Well,
How about:
A long pole,
A lean pole,
A bamboo or
A bean pole?
A flag pole,
A tent pole,
A barber's or
A bent pole?
A green pole,
A grey pole,
A curtain or
A maypole?
A whole pole,
A half pole,
A great big
Telegraph pole?

No!
Not any sort –
No small pole,
No large pole –
I wouldn't touch it with a barge pole.

Let Basil go to Basildon

Let Basil go to Basildon,
Let Lester go to Leicester;
Let Steven go to Stevenage
With raincoat and sou'wester.

Let Peter go to Peterhead,
Let Dudley go to Dudley;
Let Milton go to Milton Keynes –
The pavements there are puddly.

Let Felix go to Felixstowe,
Let Barry go to Barry;
Let Mabel go to Mablethorpe,
But I at home shall tarry.

Let Alice go to Alice Springs,
Let Florence go to Florence;
Let Benny go to Benidorm
Where rain comes down in torrents.

Let Winnie go to Winnipeg,
Let Sidney go to Sydney;
Let Otto go to Ottawa –
I am not of that kidney.

Let Vera go to Veracruz,
Let Nancy go to Nancy,
But I'll stay home while others
  roam –
Abroad I do not fancy.

I Sometimes Wonder Whether

I sometimes wonder whether
Dear Old Mother Nature ever
Admits she makes a few mistakes,
Such as the porcupine;
And then I start to wonder
About each and every blunder,
And what I'd do to change the world,
If only it were mine.

It seems to me the puma
Doesn't have a sense of humour,
I've never seen a puma try
To make hyenas laugh;
And what about the llama,
Can his life be full of drama,
Or does he wish, as I suspect,
That he were a giraffe?

And then there are those creatures
With the funniest of features,
The mouse or moose or grouse or goose,
To mention but a few;
And bears like the koala,
I'd send to a beauty parlour,
And crocodiles and crabs, I think,
Could also join the queue!

Words with Teacher

These are the words that teachers use:
Hypothesis, hypotenuse,
Isosceles, trapezium,
Potassium, magnesium,
Denominator, catechism
And antidisestablishmentarianism.

The Cat and the King

A cat may look at a king
And a king may look at a cat.
If thin the cat and fat the king,
There isn't much danger in *that*.
But just suppose fat is the cat,
Conversely, thin the king,
The king gets mighty cross at that,
And stamps like anything.

The Wherefore and the Why

The Therefore and the Thereupon,
The Wherefore and the Why;
The Hitherto, the Whitherto,
The Thus, the Thence, the Thy.

The Whysoever, Whereupon,
The Whatsoever, Whence;
The Hereinafter, Hereupon,
The Herebefore and Hence.

The Thereby and the Thereabouts,
The Thee, the Thou, the Thine;
I don't care for their whereabouts,
And they don't care for mine!

To Be a Bee?

To be a bee or not to be
A bee, that is the question.
You see, I'm in a quandary.
'To be a bee or not to be
A bee' is what perplexes me,
Pray, what is your suggestion?
To be a bee or not to be
A bee, that is the question.

Longwindedness and What it Boils Down to

Would you kindly care to join me
In a game of table tennis?
(For it will be so exciting,
'Dorothea versus Dennis'.)
Can we sing O *Sole Mio*
Like the gondoliers in Venice?
Dare we watch a monster movie
All about an apelike menace?

Let's watch *King Kong*, have a ding-dong
Game of ping-pong and a sing-song.

Jingle-Jangle-Jent

A Viking liking hiking walked
From Katmandu to Kent,
And Timbuctoo and Teddington
Were towns he did frequent,
And yet with everything he saw
And everywhere he went,
He never ever saw the sight
Of Jingle-Jangle-Jent;
He *never* ever saw the sight
Of Jingle-Jangle-Jent.

A Druid fond of fluid drank
More than you've ever dreamt,
It took one hundred pints of
beer
Until he was content,
And yet with all the liquid that
He to his stomach sent,
He never ever knew the taste
Of Jingle-Jangle-Jent;
He *never* ever knew the taste
Of Jingle-Jangle-Jent.

vet who let his pet get wet
n Ancient Egypt spent
Iis life with sickly squawks and
squeals,
o which his ears he lent.
Ie learned what every whimper
was,
Vhat every mumble meant,
nd yet he never heard the noise
f Jingle-Jangle-Jent;
Ie *never* ever heard the noise
f Jingle-Jangle-Jent.

A Roman roamin' round in
Rome
Aromas did invent,
By mixing potions in a pot,
As over it he bent.
His nostrils were of noble nose,
Yet it is evident,
He never ever caught the whiff
Of Jingle-Jangle-Jent;
He *never* ever caught the whiff
Of Jingle-Jangle-Jent.

Me and Amanda

Me
and
Amanda
meander,
like
rivers
that
run
to
the
sea.
We
wander
at
random
we're
always
in
tandem:
meandering
Mandy
and
me.

An Understanding Man

I have an understanding
With an understanding man:
His umbrella I stand under
When I understand I can.

Old Shivermetimbers

Old Shivermetimbers, the Sea-faring Cat,
Was born on the edge of the ocean,
And his days (just to prove that the world isn't flat)
Are spent in perpetual motion.

Old Shivermetimbers, the Nautical Cat,
Has seen every port of the atlas;
First feline, he was, to set foot in Rabat,
A place which was hitherto catless.

Old Shivermetimbers, the Sea-faring Cat,
Has numbered as seventy-seven
The times that he's chartered the cold Kattegat
And steered by the stars up in Heaven.

Old Shivermetimbers, the Nautical Cat,
Loves the scent of the sea on his whiskers,
So it isn't surprising to hear him say that
He don't give a hoot for hibiscus.

Old Shivermetimbers, the Sea-faring Cat,
Has travelled aboard the *Queen Mary*,
Though I saw him last Saturday queuing up at
Calais, for the cross-Channel ferry.

Old Shivermetimbers, the Nautical Cat,
Has spent his whole life on the ocean,
Yet how he acquired that old admiral's hat,
I honestly haven't a notion.

Poems to Ponder

The Silent Ship

I sailed a ship as white as snow,
As soft as clouds on high,
Tall was the mast, broad was the beam,
And safe and warm was I.

I stood astern my stately ship
And felt so grand and high,
To see the lesser ships give way
As I went gliding by.

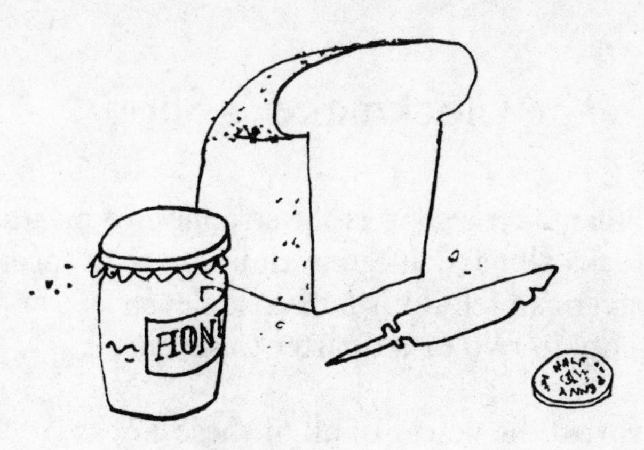

Half Measures

If I had a half a penny,
I would buy a half a loaf
And a half a pound of honey
And a half a silver knife.

Oh, I wouldn't half be happy
As the half a loaf I slice,
And I'd spread on half the honey
With my half a silver knife.

And a half of it would fill me,
And a half would fill my wife;
Oh, we wouldn't half be full up,
And it wouldn't half be nice.

But I haven't half a penny,
So I haven't half a knife,
Or a half a loaf and honey,
And I haven't half a wife.

The Clockmaker's Shop

The clockmaker's shop is the strangest of places,
The clocks all have different times on their faces;
You never can tell if it's half past eleven
Or twenty to two or a quarter to seven.

How varied the voices of all of these clocks,
Oh, what a collection of ticketytocks!
Some with a heartbeat that seems in a flurry,
And some with a heart that refuses to hurry.

Some of them tinkle away like rain water,
And some of them strike on the dot every quarter;
Some of them sound with a simple ding-dong,
And some with a rather superior song.

Some have a sound that won't stir you in bed,
And some have alarms that could wake up the dead;
Some have a chapel-like bell of a chime,
And one has a cuckoo to tell you the time!

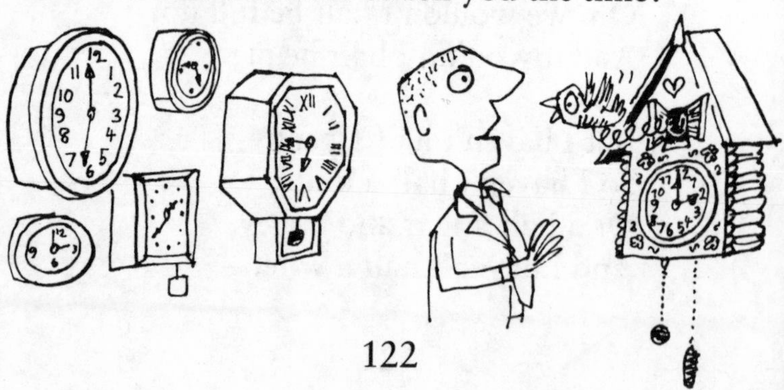

The Father Christmas on the Cake

For fifty weeks I've languished
Upon the cupboard shelf,
Forgotten and uncared for,
I've muttered to myself.
But now the year is closing,
And Christmastime is here,
They dust me down and tell me
To show a little cheer.
Between the plaster snowman
And little glassy lake
They stand me in the middle
Of some ice-covered cake,
And for a while there's laughter,
But as the week wears on,
They cut up all the landscape
Till every scrap is gone.
Then with the plaster snowman
And little lake of glass
I'm banished to the cupboard
For one more year to pass.

Over the Orchard Wall

Over the orchard wall we'd go,
And Tom was always first,
For there grew cherries, plums and pears
To quench a summer thirst.
'It's pears and plums for me!' cried Tom,
And shook them from the tree,
While I picked cherries from a bough
To take to Rose-Marie.

But then one day, old Farmer Jones
Came by and caught us out,
And, as he chased us from his land,
I'm sure I heard him shout:
'Be off with you, you greedy boys,
For I've a family
Who must be fed – a wife, a son,
And daughter Rose-Marie.'

Rosemary's Friends

O, Rosemary's friends are her mantelshelf folk:
A shepherd, two sweethearts, a milkmaid with
 yoke,
And grandest of all is a cricketer chap
Who stands at the wicket in flannels and cap,
Awaiting a ball that's about to be bowled,
For years he's been batting – no wonder he's
 old;
But happy is Rosie to have such a man
And yesterday morning she told me her plan:
'I'm off to have tea with W. G. Grace
And polish the porcelain beard on his face.'

The Lost Ball

My sister hit our tennis ball
Right over next door's garden wall.
Our neighbour's name is Mr Hall,
A grumpy man who's rather small.
But unlike him, his garden wall
Must stand a hundred inches tall.
It's no use to go round and call
And ask him to return our ball,
(For he's the sort who hoards each ball
Which happens on his lawn to fall.)
Nor can we climb his garden wall,
And there's no gap through which to crawl.
There seems to be no chance at all
That we'll retrieve our tennis ball.
But wait, what's this? Our tennis ball!
Oh, thank you kindly, Mr Hall!

The Ladybird Traveller

You've heard of a Bee in the Bonnet,
You've heard of a Fly on the Wall,
Well, I am a Ladybird Traveller,
Who travels the world at a crawl.

Frontiers for me aren't a problem
I pass over mountains with ease,
I can stroll round the world in an hour
And cross all the Seven High Seas.

The Tropics, the Poles, the Equator,
I can visit them all in a day:
An afternoon spent in the Indies,
An evening spent in Cathay.

Africa, Asia and Europe,
My world is a peaceable place,
But should I one day find it tiresome,
I shall simply fly off into space.

The Violin-fiddle

The violin is highly strung
And melancholy is her song,
But should she choose to change her tune,
She'll fiddle 'neath a gypsy moon.

Going to the Bank

When Uncle Ben goes to the bank,
I like to go there too,
But not for business purposes
As other people do.

I go to see the blotting pad
Which on the counter lies –
For there I know I'll find a treat
On which to feast my eyes.

For everything is back to front
In Blotting Paper Land –
Men's signatures and ladies' names
Writ in a magic hand!

Mere words become weird alphabets
Of dashes and of dots,
And who can guess what sorcery
Lies hidden in the blots?

And when I'm older, will *I* make
Strange marks on paper pink,
And leave behind *my* magic spell
In backward-slanting ink?

Commonsense

If Commonsense were sold in shops,
I'd purchase me a pound:

I'd give a quarter
To Sir John,

A quarter
To Miss Brown,

A quarter to
Old Algernon,

A quarter to
His hound.

And all the Commonsense left over,
I'd put it on the shelf,
Wrapped in a cotton handkerchief,
And keep it for myself.

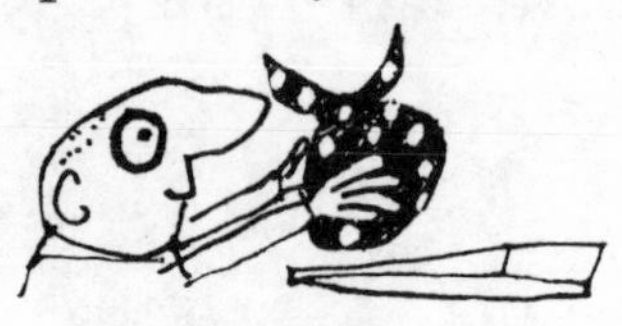

A Scarecrow Remembers

Head of straw and heart of wood,
With arms outstretched like this I've stood
For half a year in Hertfordshire,
My feet stuck in the mud.

Things could be worse, for I remember
One day early in November,
The children came from far and wide
Wheeling a barrow with another
Ragged fellow flopped inside.
But no sooner had I glimpsed my brother
Than they took him from his carriage
To a hilltop where they perched him on a pyre,
And they laughed to watch him perish
As they set his clothes on fire.

The sky that night was filled with light,
With shooting stars and rockets,
I stood my ground and made no sound
When sparks fell in my pockets.

Amidst the Bedlam I could see
Old Owl a-tremble in his tree,
And when the noise at last died down
The children all returned to town,
And left the bonfire smouldering,
And my poor brother mouldering,
Till only ash remained.

My Cat

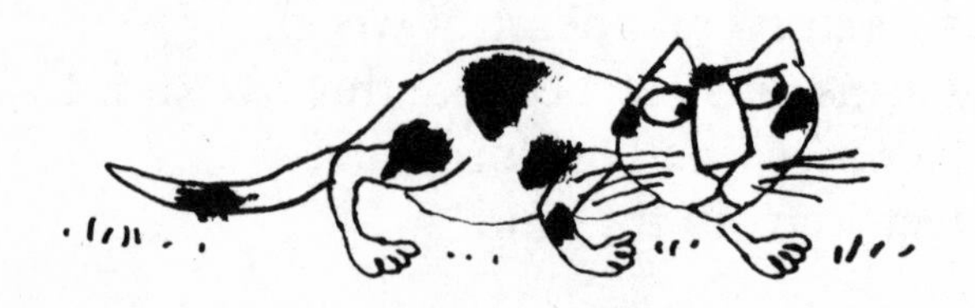

My cat can stalk,
My cat can prance,
My cat can skip,
My cat can dance.

My cat can yawn,
My cat can purr,
My cat can preen
His silky fur.

My cat can leap,
My cat can pounce,
My cat can bound,
My cat can bounce.

My cat can taunt,
My cat can tease,
My cat can hide
In boughs of trees.

My cat can plod,
My cat can prowl,
My cat can scratch,
My cat can growl.

My cat can do
Just anything,
But catch a bird
That's on the wing.

Rainbow Ship

Two dreams I've always cherished:
To sail upon the main,
And to regard a rainbow
Without a drop of rain.

That rainbow seemed elusive,
I never sailed the sea,
Until Uncle Horatio
A present gave to me:

A Ship Inside a Bottle!
Now in its glassy realm,
My little ship goes sailing,
With me stood at the helm.

And when the sun is shining
Upon the glass, I've found,
Without a single raindrop,
A rainbow's all around.

The Moon

The moon, she came in through my window,
When everyone else was asleep;
Her silvery light made everything bright
As softly she started to creep.

And once round my room the moon travelled
As over my pillow she passed,
And every dark nook and picture and book
Came under the gaze that she cast.

Then when she was through with exploring,
She left me without a 'goodbye',
And when she was gone, I felt quite alone
To see her returned to the sky.

Hopeless
History

King Solomon

King
Solomon
was
seldom
sad
when
climbing
up
a
column,
but
when
he
started
sliding
down,
King
Solomon
was
solemn!

Nero

Nero, plump about the middle,
Played requests upon the fiddle.
The most engaging tune he played
Was for the local fire brigade.

Boadicea

When Boadicea was on the road,
She didn't heed the Highway Code,
And if she met a Roman crew,
Cried, 'Fancy running into you!'

King Arthur's Knights

King Arthur's knights were chivalrous
When sat around his table,
But even they were frivolous
Whenever they were able,
And in the moat at Camelot
They splashed about and swam a lot.

Alfred the Great

Alfred the Great was a hero,
But heroes can still make mistakes.
He didn't watch fires like Nero,
And ended up burning the cakes.

Columbus

Columbus very well knew that
The world was round, it wasn't flat,
And almost went hysterical
Just proving it was spherical.

Elizabeth I

Elizabeth the First, I hear,
Was quite a fussy queen,
And had a hot bath once a year
To keep her body clean.

Raleigh and Elizabeth

When Raleigh met Elizabeth,
And it was rather muddy,
He wouldn't let her feet get wet,
He *was* a fuddy-duddy.

So he laid down his velvet cloak,
The Queen, she didn't falter.
She thought it odd, but on it trod,
And said, 'Arise, Sir Walter.'

Sir Isaac Newton

Sir Isaac Newton liked to grapple
With problems astronomical.
Then on his head there fell an apple,
Which may strike you as comical.
But for Sir Isaac 'twas to be
A matter of some gravity.

Napoleon

Napoleon Bonaparte
Was never alone, apart
From when he'd tell his queen:
'Not tonight, Josephine.'

George Washington

George Washington chopped down a tree
And couldn't tell a lie;
When questioned by his father, he
Confessed, 'Yes, it was I.'

But as he handed back the axe,
He added in defence:
'Good training, sir, for lumberjacks
Or would-be presidents.'

Einstein

Long years ago, nobody cared
That E was really mc^2.
Then Albert Einstein thought a bit,
And felt that he should mention it.

A Survey of Sovereigns

William, William, Henry the First,
Stephen and Henry the Second;

Richard and John, sir, and Henry the Third,
Then one, two, three Edwards, 'tis reckoned.

Richard the Second and Henry the Fourth,
And Henrys the Fifth and the Sixth, sir;

Edward the Fourth and young Edward the Fifth,
Then Richard or Crooked King Dick, sir.

Henry the Seventh and Henry the Eighth,
Then Edward, then Mary was queen, sir.

Elizabeth, James, then Kings Charles One
and Two,
(With Oliver Cromwell between, sir).

James, William & Mary, then following Anne,
Four Georges, one after another;

Then William, Victoria, Edward and George
To Edward, who said, 'Crown my brother.'

Stories in Stanzas

The Saddest Spook

The saddest spook there ever was
Is melancholious because
He can't so much as raise a sneer,
Or laugh a laugh that's vaguely queer.

He hasn't learnt to walk through walls,
And dares not answer wolfish calls,
And when big ghosts are rude and coarse,
And shout at him: 'Your fangs are false,'

He smiles at them, just like a fool,
But wishes they'd pick on a ghoul
Who's heavyweight and not just bantam,
Why pick on a little phantom?

The Lighthouse Keeper

I met the lighthouse
keeper's wife,
His nephew, niece,
and daughter;
His uncle and his
auntie too,
When I went 'cross
the water.

I met the lighthouse
keeper's son,
His father and his
mother;
His grandpa and his
grandma too,
His sister and his
brother.

I met the lighthouse
keeper's mate,
Who, running out
of patience,
Told me, 'The keeper's
gone ashore
To round up more
relations.'

My Sister is Missing

Harriet, Harriet, jump on your chariot,
My sister is missing, poor Janet!
And Michael, O Michael, go pedal your cycle,
And search every part of the planet.

My sister, my sister, since breakfast I've missed her,
I'll never grow used to the silence;
So Cecil, O Cecil, I'm glad you can wrestle,
For Janet is prone to use violence.

With Doris and Maurice and Horace and Boris
We'll follow the points of the compass,
And if we should find her, we'll creep up behind her,
But quietly, for Janet might thump us.

We'll hold her and scold her until we have told her
That running away isn't funny;
But if she says sorry, we'll hire a big lorry,
And drive off to somewhere that's sunny.

We'll wander and ponder in fields over yonder,
But wait! What's that dot in the distance?
It looks like a figure, it's getting much bigger,
It's shouting at all my assistants.

O Janet, my Janet, it can't be, or can it?
My sister is no longer missing!
Hooray! We have found her, let's gather around her,
Let's start all the hugging and kissing!

A Blackpool Ballad

At *Two Fat Ladies* Tower View
Lived lonely lovelorn Dick,
Who loved a girl along the way
At number *Clickety Click*.

Sue was the lass from Lancashire
He'd loved since he was seven:
He loved her hair, he loved her eyes,
He loved her *Legs Eleven*.

But Sue, she loved a lad called Jim,
Who worked the Bingo Hall;
Each night till half past *Maggie's Den*
She'd listen to him call.

One night, when Dick saw them embrace,
With rage he shook his fist,
For Susan, who was *Sweet Sixteen*,
He thought had ne'er been kissed.

Cried Dick to Jim, 'Let go of her!
Sweet Sue, I love thee more.
Please take, now I am come of age,
My own *Key of the Door*.'

Jim laughed aloud at such a vow
And sneered, 'I'm sorry, mate,
But I'm the *Kelly's Eye* for Sue –
We've fixed upon a date!'

As poor heart-broken Dick sloped off
Across the prom from Jim,
A Number Thirteen tram appeared –
Unlucky 'twas for him.

* * *

They buried Dick beneath the sands,
And as the mourners passed,
Sighed Sue, 'Love's like a Bingo Game,
His number's up at last.'

Martha's Hair

In January Martha's hair
Was like the wild mane of a mare.
In February Martha thought
Just for a change she'd cut it short.

In March my Martha dyed it red
And stacked it high upon her head.
In April Martha changed her mind
And wore a pony tail behind.

Come May she couldn't care a fig
And shaved her head and wore a wig.
In June, when it had grown once more,
A yellow ribbon Martha wore.

And in July, like other girls,
My Martha was a mass of curls.
In August, having tired of that,
She combed it out and brushed it flat.

September saw my Martha's hair
With streaks of silver here and there.
And in October, just for fun,
On top she tied it in a bun.

November Martha chose to spend
Making her hair stand up on end.
And by December, Martha's mane
Had grown unruly once again.

Charlie's Cherry Tree

very summer Charlie waited
y his Cherry Tree;
herries grew and Charlie picked them,
ad them for his tea.

hen one summer Charlie waited,
herries didn't grow;
harlie waited for a long time,
herries didn't show.

All through summer Charlie waited,
Autumn, winter, spring;
Charlie waited for a whole year,
Didn't get a thing.

Charlie mad and Charlie angry,
Charlie took an axe;
Charlie chopped his Cherry Tree down,
Only took two whacks.

ith the wood then Charlie chiselled,
harlie made a chair;
ow he sits and Charlie wonders
hat he's doing there.

harlie sad and Charlie sorry,
harlie wishes he
adn't been so hasty chopping
own his Cherry Tree.

Humphrey Hughes of Highbury

Young Humphrey Hughes of Highbury
Goes to his local library;
They stamp his books, he softly speaks,
'I'll bring them back within three weeks.'
He always looks so meek and mild
That grown-ups think, 'There goes a child
Who'll grow into a charming youth.'
But little do they know the truth.

For when he's home, young Humphrey Hughes
Forgets to ever wipe his shoes,
And at his mother merely sneers
As to his room he disappears.
When there his library books he takes,
His body with excitement shakes,
For Humphrey so enjoys himself
When placing books upon his shelf.

But there upon his shelf they stay,
Untouched, unread, until the day
He takes one down and with a grin
Looks at the date that's stamped within.

With laughter he begins to shriek,
For all his books were due last week.
He then decides the thing to do
Is wait another week or two.

So time goes by until, at last,
When six or seven weeks have passed,
There comes the knock upon the door
That Humphrey has been waiting for.
His mother gets a nasty shock
When answering the caller's knock,
For there she finds two boys in blue –
In search of books long overdue.

But, pleading absentmindedness,
Young Hughes could simply not care less,
And so, with some reluctancy,
The constables accept his plea.
They take the long-lost books away,
But warn he'll have a fine to pay,
Yet Humphrey merely looks benign,
For Mummy always pays the fine!

The Missing Eskimo

There is an igloo far away
Without an Eskimo;
Now, could a blizzard yesterday
Have buried him in snow?

Or did he in his kayak go
Till he could go no more,
And so today our Eskimo
Sits on some foreign shore?

I saw a polar bear last night
Who looked a hungry beast;
Perhaps he gave our friend a fright
And made of him a feast?

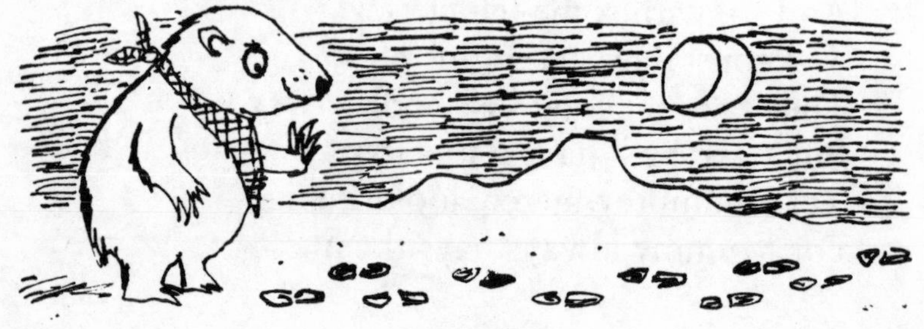

Or did he, on some distant floe
Walk where the ice was thin,
And thus our hapless Eskimo
Fell through and tumbled in?

Or on the other hand, perhaps,
He went off on his sledge,
But having crossed the Land of Lapps
Was dragged clean off the edge?

The possibilities, I'd say
Are endless. All I know
Is, there's an igloo far away
Without an Eskimo. . .

Marmaduke the Noisy Knight

In Arthur's reign or thereabouts,
When fellows drank from flagons,
A knight who knew the whereabouts
Of unicorns or dragons
Was very likely to impress
A dozen damsels in distress.

But one poor knight named Marmaduke,
Who'd never bravely battled,
Could not so much as harm a duke,
Because his armour rattled.
And when he moved, he couldn't hide
The noises coming from inside.

He never dared, like Lancelot,
Queen Guinevere to flatter,
For never could he dance a lot,
As he was bound to clatter.

And Marmaduke was most provoked
When ladies laughed and jesters joked.

At last he told a farmer off
Who ridiculed his rattle,
And then he tore his armour off
In front of all the cattle,
And as he threw it to the ground,
It gave one final clanging sound.

He then ran off, I wonder where
On earth he might have gone to?
He only had his underwear
And helmet to hang onto.
He must have made a sorry sight,
Poor Marmaduke the Noisy Knight.

Miss Evans

She dropped in for elevenses,
I heard the church bell chime
At quarter past. 'Good Heavens! Is . . .'
She muttered, 'that the time?'

I wished she'd had some previous
Engagement which was urgent,
For patenting a devious
Device to save detergent.

But no! Miss Evans couldn't care
For anything like that!
She asked me if I wouldn't care
To take her coat and hat.

She eyed my every ornament –
The cup my brother won
At some old tennis tournament.
Pray, have another bun!

I offered her Madeira cake
And coffee by the cup.
(Whenever she is near a cake
She gets the urge to sup.)

I played her some Sibelius
Upon my xylophone.
She said she favoured Delius
And scoffed a further scone.

She claimed that life's a mockery
With no one to harangue.
She claimed she liked the crockery
And took my last meringue.

She ate my salmon sandwiches
And all my apple pie.
I shook her by the hand (which is
The way to say goodbye).

She dropped in for elevenses,
But stayed to have her tea.
The thing about Miss Evans is
She 'needs the company'.

Ridiculous
Rhymes

Ask a Silly Question

Tell me how in the deep
Does the whale go to sleep,
How does he rest his poor blubber?

He lays down his head
Upon the sea bed,
And snores just like a landlubber!

Tell me why in the sky
Can an ostrich not fly,
Why can't he fly like an eagle?

Because he once heard
From some funny bird
That flying is highly illegal!

Tell me where on the earth
Does the monkey find mirth,
Where does he go to find laughter?

He climbs up a tree
To watch you and me,
Then happily lives ever after!

Jocelyn, My Dragon

My dragon's name is Jocelyn,
He's something of a joke.
For Jocelyn is very tame,
He doesn't like to maul or maim,
Or breathe a fearsome fiery flame;
He's much too smart to smoke.

And when I take him to the park
The children form a queue,
And say, 'What lovely eyes of red!'
As one by one they pat his head.
And Jocelyn is so well-bred,
He only eats a few!

Who?

Who's always there come rain or shine,
From eight o'clock till ten past nine?
Who's back again at half past three
As we are going home for tea?
Who wears a coat that's long and white,
And cap with badge that's big and bright?
Who's always cheerful, always nice?
Whose banner bears a strange device?
Who teaches us the Highway Code,
And sees us safely 'cross the road?
Who is it makes the traffic stop?
O Lady of the Lollipop!

The New Boy

Please, sir, I'm the new boy,
My trousers are corduroy,
My cap's the wrong colour,
My name is James Fuller.

I'm no good at games, sir,
But can tell you the names, sir,
Of all of our kings, sir,
From Norman to Windsor.

I have a pet hamster,
My mother's from Amster-
Dam, but my father's
As English as Arthur's.

I've brought a packed lunch,
  sir,
An apple to munch, sir,
Ham rolls and a number
Of cheese and cucumber.

I sang in the choir, sir,
When my voice was higher, sir,
But now that I've spoken,
You'll notice it's broken.

Please, sir, I'm the new boy,
My trousers are corduroy,
My cap's the wrong colour,
My name is James Fuller . . .

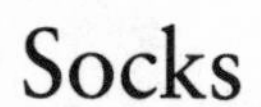

Socks

My local Gents' Outfitter stocks
The latest line in snazzy socks:
Black socks, white socks,
Morning, noon and night socks,
Grey socks, green socks,
Small, large and in between socks,
Blue socks, brown socks,
Always-falling-down socks,
Orange socks, red socks,
Baby socks and bed socks;
Purple socks, pink socks,
What-would-people-think socks,
Holey socks and frayed socks,
British Empire-made socks,
Long socks, short socks,
Any-sort-of-sport socks,
Thick socks, thin socks,
And 'these-have-just-come-in' socks.

Socks with stripes and socks with spots,
Socks with stars and polka dots,
Socks for ankles, socks for knees,
Socks with twelve-month guarantees,
Socks for aunties, socks for uncles,
Socks to cure you of carbuncles,
Socks for nephews, socks for nieces,
Socks that won't show up their creases,
Socks whose colour glows fluorescent,
Socks for child or adolescent,

ocks for ladies, socks for gents,
ocks for only fifty pence.

ocks for winter, socks for autumn,
ocks with garters to support 'em.
ocks for work and socks for leisure,
ocks hand-knitted, made-to-measure,
ocks of wool and polyester,
ocks from Lincoln, Leeds and Leicester,
ocks of cotton and elastic,
ocks of paper, socks of plastic,
ocks of silk-embroidered satin,
ocks with mottoes done in Latin,
ocks for soldiers in the army,
ocks to crochet or macramé,
ocks for destinations distant,
hrink-proof, stretch-proof, heat-resistant.

aggy socks, brief socks,
Jnion Jack motif socks,
hequered socks, tartan socks,
chool or kindergarten socks,
ensible socks, silly socks,
rivolous and frilly socks,
mpractical socks, impossible socks,
)rip-dry machine-only-washable socks,
ulgarian socks, Brazilian socks,
here seem to be over a million socks!

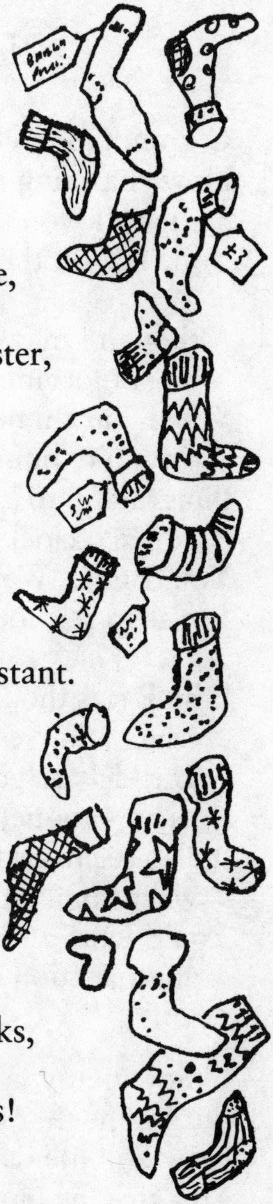

Vith all these socks, there's just one catch –
t's hard to find a pair that match.

Grandfather Clock

O grandfather clock, dear old grandfather clock,
How charming to hear is your tick and your tock;
So upright you stand day and night in the hall,
Your feet on the ground and your back to the wall.

Although I may grumble
most mornings at eight,
When you chime, 'Hurry up,
or you're bound to be late,'
I'm grateful to greet you
at five o'clock when
You chime, 'Welcome home,
nice to see you again.'

I think it is thoughtless
when relatives speak
And rudely refer to you
as an antique;
It also seems heartless
when sometimes they say
You'd fetch a fair price
at an auction one day.

I know that you're old and inclined to be slow,
But I hope that they never decide you should go.
How dull life would be if they took you away:
You give me much more than the time of the day.

Park Regulations

The rules upon this board displayed
Are here by all to be obeyed:

Keep off the grass. Don't scale the wall.
Don't throw, or kick, or bat a ball.
Don't pluck the flowers from their bed.
Don't feed the ducks with crusts of bread.
Bicycles may not be ridden.
Rollerskating is forbidden.
Dogs must be kept upon their leashes
And kept from chasing other species.
Dispose of litter thoughtfully.
Do not attempt to climb a tree
Or carve initials on the bark.
Don't play a wireless in the park
(Or any sort of instrument).
Don't build a fire or pitch a tent
And don't throw stones or gather sticks.
The gates are closed at half past six.

Observe these rules and regulations
(Signed) Head of Parks and Recreations.

The Bridle and the Saddle

The bridle and the saddle
Fitted, I sit in the middle
Of the horse, but why I straddle
Such a creature is a riddle.

O, he's big and I am little,
And he no doubt thinks I'm idle,
And he knows my bones be brittle
As I hang on to the bridle.

But it doesn't seem to addle
Him that I am in a muddle
As I cower in the saddle
When we pass over each puddle.

Don't Look in the Mirror, Maud

, don't look in the mirror, Maud,
fear that you might crack it.
new one I could not afford,
nless I sold my jacket.

nd if I sold my jacket, Maud,
could no longer wear it;
nd then I couldn't go abroad –
m sure I couldn't bear it.

or if I couldn't travel, Maud,
d never go to Venice;
d have to stay behind with Claud,
nd practise playing tennis.

nd if he were to ask me, Maud,
we could play mixed doubles,
e'd thereby contribute toward
ly many other troubles.

or if we played mixed doubles, Maud,
ith Vivian and Vera,
hey'd dress me up just like a lord
efore that very mirror.

nd if 'twere broke, they'd be appalled,
nd hit me with my racket;
don't look in the mirror, Maud,
fear that you might crack it.

Old Song Revisited

It was a feline fiddler
Who played a merry tune
Inspired a bovine acrobat
To leap over the moon;
A canine witness was amused
At shows of such buffoon-
Ery; a piece of crockery
Eloped with what? A spoon!

Leaflets

Leaflets, leaflets, I like leaflets,
love leaflets when they're free.
When I see a pile of leaflets,
take one, or two (or three).

Banks are always good for leaflets –
They've got lots of leaflets there –
Leaflets on investing money:
How to be a Millionaire.

And I go to my Gas Show Room,
For their leaflets are such fun,
And I visit travel agents –
They've got leaflets by the ton.

Leaflets, leaflets, I like leaflets,
love leaflets when they're free.
When I see a pile of leaflets,
Something strange comes over me.

Theatre foyers offer leaflets:
What to see and how to book.
Stations, libraries and so on –
All have leaflets if you look.

've got leaflets by the dozen,
've got leaflets by the score,
've got leaflets by the hundred,
Yet I always yearn for more.

A Hat

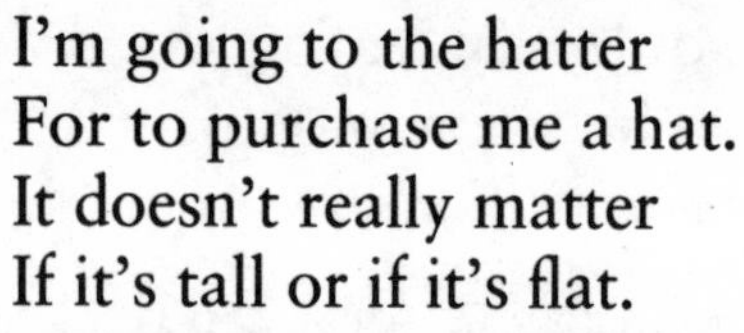

I'm going to the hatter
For to purchase me a hat.
It doesn't really matter
If it's tall or if it's flat.

I don't mind if it's black or brown
Or if it has a crumpled crown,
Or if the brim is up or down;
A simple hat is all I ask,
To cover up my ears.

I don't ask for a bonnet
That is made of velveteen,
With a lot of ribbons on it
That are yellow, pink or green.

I don't ask for a hat of crêpe,
Or one of an exotic shape,
Or one that's all tied up with tape;
A simple hat is all I ask,
To cover up my ears.

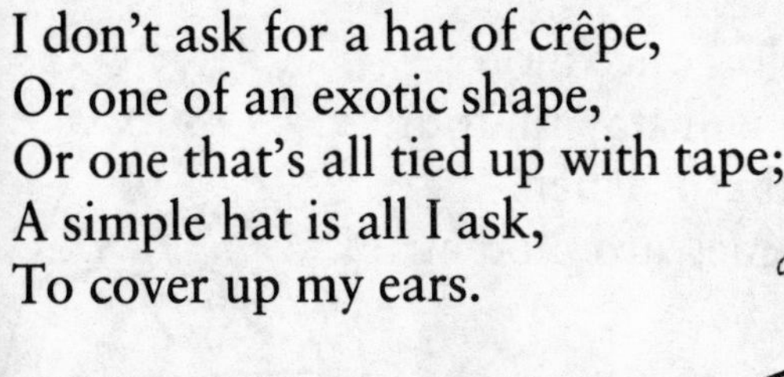

I don't want one with feathers,
Or with cherries ripe and red,
A plain hat for all weathers
Would be fine for me instead.

I do not really mind a bit
If my hat's not a *perfect* fit,
If I can just get into it,
A simple hat is all I ask,
To cover up my ears.

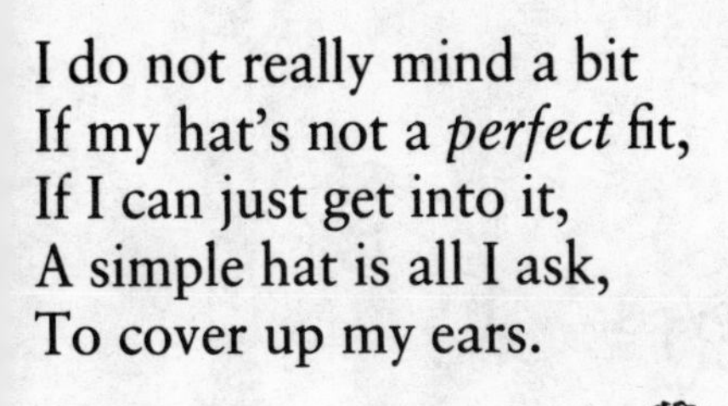

Plodders

We homeward plod, our satchels full
Of books to make our evenings dull.
We homeward plod, our heads hung low,
Crammed full of facts One Ought to Know.

Tomorrow we will plod once more
To school, where we will stay till four,
Or thereabouts, for that is when,
With books, we'll homeward plod again.

The Good, the Bored and the Ugly

A coachload of pupils
Get into their places –
The ones in the back seats
Make ugly grimaces.

The ones in the front seats
Are fairer of feature –
Directing the driver
And talking to Teacher.

The ones in the middle –
Halfway down the bus,
Just look bored and wonder,
'Oh, why all the fuss?'

The End

Index of titles & first lines